Silver Dolphins

SECRET FRIENDS

For Lee - a magical friend

First published in paperback by HarperCollins *Children's Books* in 2009

HarperCollins *Children's Books* is a division of HarperCollins *Publishers* Ltd,
77-85 Fulham Palace Road, Hammersmith, London W6 8JB.

Visit our website at: www.harpercollins.co.uk

1 3 5 7 9 10 8 6 4 2
ISBN-13: 978-0-00-730969-6

Printed and bound in England by Clays Ltd, St Ives plc

Mixed Sources
Product group from well-managed
forests and other controlled sources
www.fsc.org Cert no. SW-COC-1806
© 1996 Forest Stewardship Council
FSC

FSC is a non-profit international organisation established to promote the
responsible management of the world's forests. Products carrying the FSC
label are independently certified to assure consumers that they come
from forests that are managed to meet the social, economic and
ecological needs of present and future generations.

Find out more about HarperCollins and the environment at
www.harpercollins.co.uk/green

by Summer Waters

Silver Dolphins

SECRET FRIENDS

HarperCollins *Children's Books*

Prologue

Out at sea, two dolphins swam side by side in a comfortable silence. The larger dolphin, a handsome male with a striking yellow blaze stretched along his flank, had a far away look in his eyes. But his peace was short lived. Suddenly two smaller dolphins swam up, their voices ringing out in angry squeaks.

"Bubbles, Dream, what's all the noise about?" asked Spirit.

"It's her fault," clicked Bubbles. "I told her a secret and now she's going to tell it to the rest of the pod."

Dream flushed as Spirit regarded her with solemn eyes.

"Is this true?" he asked.

"It was a joke," clicked Dream, quietly. "I wasn't really going to tell."

"I should hope not," said Spirit. "Sharing a secret with a friend is a very special thing. You should never betray their trust."

"I know, Dad." Dream bowed her head. "I promise I wouldn't have told."

"Good," said Spirit, tapping her affectionately with his fin. "Play nicely now, my children. You can when you try."

As Bubbles and Dream swam away, Spirit turned to his wife.

"They could be really good friends if they didn't argue so much."

Smiling wistfully, Star answered, "It's all part of growing up."

"Yes," clicked Spirit, thoughtfully. "They have lots to learn, just like our new Silver Dolphin."

"The Silver Dolphin learns quickly," clicked Star. "We are lucky to have found her."
Spirit nodded his magnificent silver head.

"The Silver Dolphin grows more powerful every day. With her power comes great responsibility. She still has much to learn…"

Chapter One

The wind was getting up. It ruffled the surface of the sea, whipping it into tiny white crested waves. Antonia Lee pushed her long blonde hair out of her eyes, wishing she'd thought to tie it up.

"Hurry up, Flipper Feet," called Bubbles. "We're nearly there."

He took off, leaping in and out of the water, flying over the waves with an easy grace. Antonia went after him, marvelling at the way she too could swim like a dolphin.

"I can't believe I've only been a Silver Dolphin for two weeks," she whistled.

"Me neither," Bubbles clicked back. "Your swimming's even better now. You're using your hands like flippers instead of that funny thing you did with them at first."

Antonia laughed, her voice coming out as a series of whistles.

"That was breaststroke. It's a popular swimming stroke."

"It can't be that good or dolphins would use it," Bubbles teased.

Antonia Lee was a Silver Dolphin. Silver

Dolphins were guardians of the sea. They used magic to care for the oceans and all the creatures living there. Whenever help was needed the tiny silver dolphin charm that Antonia wore round her neck called to her. Then she would take on dolphin-like characteristics enabling her to swim to the problem and sort it out. Silver Dolphins were rare. You had to be in tune with nature and willing to believe that magical things could happen to become one.

Antonia had just come out of school when Spirit called her. Spirit was the leader of a pod of thirty dolphins and he was also Bubbles's dad. Antonia answered his call quickly, but this time it wasn't an emergency. Spirit had asked Antonia to go litter-picking on the rocks. It was

Antonia's least favourite task, but a very important one. Litter could cause all sorts of injuries to sea life. When the litter-picking was finished Antonia was allowed to play with Bubbles, her best dolphin friend.

"We're here," said Bubbles, swimming round the headland.

Antonia slowed, gasping with delight at the tiny cove nestling between the rocks.

"I never knew that this was here," she clicked.

"That's because you can't reach it by land," said Bubbles. "Come on, I'll race you."

Bubbles took off, slicing through the water like a silver arrow. Antonia chased after him, determined to catch him up, but not quite making it.

"Cheat!" she clicked as Bubbles reached the

mouth of the cove a tail length ahead of her. "You had a head start."

Playfully she splashed water at him. Bubbles smacked the sea with his tail, soaking Antonia back.

"Water fight," he whistled in delight.

Antonia churned up the sea with her hands while Bubbles retaliated with his tail and flippers. Soon they could hardly see each other for the spray.

"Truce," clicked Antonia, gasping for breath.

Bubbles stopped splashing and dived under water. Antonia lay on her back staring up at the grey sky. It was a chilly start to the week following on from a scorching hot weekend. Antonia tensed as her body started to tingle. Something was approaching. She could feel the vibrations in the water. She rolled over and scanned the horizon. A dolphin was swimming towards them. As it drew closer Antonia saw it was larger than Bubbles and the blaze of yellow along its flank was much paler.

"Dream!" she exclaimed, immediately recognising Bubbles's older sister. "Look, Bubbles, your sister is—"

She didn't get to finish as something butted her in the back then ducked her under the water.

"Got you!" whistled Bubbles cheekily as Antonia spluttered to the surface. Then splashing her with a flipper, he launched straight into another water fight.

"Whoah!" cried Antonia, pointing at Dream, but Bubbles hadn't seen his sister

14

arriving and was enjoying himself far too much to stop.

"Bubbles!" clicked Dream angrily as she got caught up in the spray. "Stop that now or I'm telling Mum."

Bubbles jumped in surprise, then, quickly recovering, he splashed Dream with his tail.

"Spoilsport," he retorted.

"Stop it!" said Dream crossly. "Mum and Dad have been looking everywhere for you. You've got to come back to the pod. Dad says a storm's brewing so we're all moving out to sea where it'll be safer."

"Is it a bad storm?" asked Antonia, trying to ignore Bubbles, who had stopped splashing and was mimicking the serious expression on his sister's face. She wished the two dolphins got on better. Antonia was longing to make friends with Dream but the older dolphin never wanted to play if Bubbles was there.

"Bad enough," said Dream. "Can't you feel how the wind's getting up?"

Antonia had noticed the wind and now she thought about it she had a vague feeling that something wasn't right. She concentrated on the feeling and her sense of unease grew stronger. Antonia shivered, hoping that nothing bad was going to happen.

"I'd better go home too," she said. "It's nearly my tea time."

"I wish you could come out to sea with us," said Bubbles.

"So do I." Antonia rubbed her nose against Bubbles's nose. "Be safe."

"You too, Silver Dolphin," said Bubbles, rubbing her back.

Antonia swam with Bubbles and Dream as far as the headland then, using her legs like a tail, she trod water, watching the dolphins as they continued out to sea. After a while they turned. Bubbles leapt a somersault and Dream half bowed then together they dived out of sight. Forlornly Antonia stared at the empty sea until remembering her own family, she cheered up. It would have been nice to go with the dolphins, but she had her own home. Her parents and little sister Jessica would miss her terribly if she didn't return and she would miss her family too. Antonia swam into Gull Bay and when the water was shallow enough she stopped swimming and paddled through the breakers. Her legs no longer felt melded together and the salty water poured off her like a fountain. By the time she reached the spot on the beach where she'd left her shoes, socks and school bag the only thing to show that she'd been swimming with the dolphins was her slightly damp hair. Antonia stuffed her socks into her school bag, slid her feet into the sandals and shouldering her bag, made for the tiny track that led home.

Jessica pounced on her the moment she walked through the door.

"You've been ages. Was it really busy at Sea Watch? I wish I was big enough to help too."

Sea Watch was a local charity involved in marine conservation. It was run by an old lady called Claudia Neal. Claudia had been a Silver

Dolphin once, but it was too much for her now so she'd handed the role over to Antonia. Most days Antonia went to Sea Watch after school to help out, but today she'd gone to answer Spirit's call instead.

"Sea Watch is always busy," said Antonia, answering Jessica's question as truthfully as she could. Claudia hadn't told her that being a Silver Dolphin had to be kept secret, but Antonia knew it did. The best magic always was.

After an enormous tea of macaroni cheese, crispy bacon and broccoli followed by a dish of ice cream Antonia allowed Jessica to drag her off to her bedroom to play at being vets. Jessica got all her cuddly toys out of the wardrobe and the two girls spent the evening bandaging paws and tails. At last Mrs Lee rescued Antonia by chivvying Jessica off to have her bath.

Relieved to finally have some time alone Antonia made her way to her cosy attic bedroom. Someone, probably Mum, had opened the sloping window that looked out across Gull Bay. The salty wind rushed in, its chilly fingers lifting the pages of the wildlife magazine lying on her desk. Antonia pulled the window shut and stood for a moment staring into the light summer evening. The bay was empty. Where were the dolphins? Had Spirit taken them a very long way out to sea? Antonia could sense the impending storm more keenly now. She could smell it: a sharp tangy smell that lingered in her nose and made her muscles tingle with anticipation. Fingering the silver dolphin charm hanging round her neck, Antonia hoped that her dolphins were safe.

Chapter Two

ntonia woke with a start. She couldn't see a thing, her room was blacker than a witch's hat, but she had no difficulty hearing the storm raging outside. The wind shrieked and rain drummed on her window, sounding like pebbles being thrown against the glass. Sleepily Antonia touched her silver dolphin charm, loving the way it felt as soft as a real dolphin. She wondered what the dolphins were doing now. She hoped they were safely out at sea, dozing. Dolphins didn't fall asleep like other animals – they had to keep half awake or they would drown. Antonia closed her eyes and was almost asleep when a loud crack woke her. Having lived all her life in their little house overlooking the sea, Antonia was very familiar with that sound. It was a distress flare. Immediately she was out of bed and pulling up the blind to peer through the slanting window.

Another crack rent the night air and this time Antonia saw a spiralling plume of red smoke away to her left over Sandy Bay. Hoping that the lifeboat crew would rescue whoever was in danger Antonia crawled back to bed.

She slept soundly until Jessica roared in and shook her awake.

"Get up," she cried excitedly. "We're on the news. Sandy Bay's on television!"

"Whaa…" mumbled Antonia, pulling the duvet over her head to blot out Jessica's shrill voice.

Jessica gripped the duvet and tugged it back. "There's this boat. The *Princess Romana*. It got grounded in the storm and lost its cargo. Millions of boxes. And it's all washing up on Sandy Bay beach. Hurry or you'll miss it."

Antonia followed Jessica downstairs and into the kitchen where Mum and Dad were watching the local news on television. A picture of Sandy Bay filled the screen and

Antonia gasped at the sight of so many crates littering the shore line.

"The Italian cargo ship, *Princess Romana*, suffered some damage when it grounded and there's been a slight oil spill," said the news reporter, sounding grave. "It's not serious and marine experts say the oil should disperse on its own; however, they are keeping an eye on the situation. Several oiled birds have already been found on the beach and are being dealt with by Sea Watch, a local charity for marine conservation."

"Oh, those poor birds!"

As the picture switched back to the television studio Antonia turned to her mum and dad.

"Claudia's going to need help. Can I have

the day off school and go to Sea Watch instead?"

"No," said Mum and Dad together.

"But Claudia needs me," said Antonia, lightly touching her silver dolphin charm.

"There'll be plenty of time to help at Sea Watch after school," said Mum firmly. "Claudia wouldn't want you to skip lessons."

"*Pleeeease,*" wheedled Antonia. "Just for today."

"No," said Mum, sounding cross. "You spend quite enough time at Sea Watch as it is. We hardly see you these days. Now go and get dressed. Breakfast is ready."

Antonia was desperate to help at Sea Watch, but when Mum said no in that tone of voice she meant it. Disappointed, she went upstairs to dress.

It was a beautiful morning and Antonia could hardly believe that a few hours ago everything was being battered by the wind and rain. The air smelt clean and fresh and the early morning sun warmed Antonia's face and legs as she walked round to Sophie's house. Sophie was Antonia's oldest friend and they always walked to school together. Recently they'd fallen out, but it hadn't taken long for them to make up again. Antonia was glad; she was so close to Sophie that sometimes it felt like they were sisters. Sophie was waiting at the end of her drive, her blue eyes shining with excitement. She'd seen Sandy Bay on television too and was dying to go and look at the stricken ship.

"Let's go down to the beach before school,"

she suggested. "It's almost on our way and we've heaps of time."

Antonia wanted to see the *Princess Romana* and couldn't see the harm in having a quick look. As she approached the beach she found half her school were there too; their blue and yellow Sandy Bay Primary uniforms standing out amongst the throng of sightseers. Antonia stood on the promenade gaping at the sight before her. It looked as if someone had organised a massive jumble sale on the beach. The white-gold sand was littered with all sorts of items: packets of nappies, tins of food, barrels of wine and crockery. There was even a motorbike being wheeled away by two sturdy men. People were rummaging through crates, tossing items on to the sand and stuffing others into large plastic sacks. An argument broke out between a boy and girl. Recognising the girl's voice Antonia looked closer and saw it was Lauren Hampton, the class bully. There was a mean look on Lauren's face as she wrestled a steering wheel from the hands of the boy.

"Whatever does she want with that?" giggled Sophie, following Antonia's gaze.

"I have no idea." Antonia giggled too. "It's stealing, though. There's an old law that says lost cargo has to be returned to its owner."

"Are you sure?" Sophie sounded disbelieving. "Only there's a brand-new set of paintbrushes down there I kind of had my eye on. Look, I'm going to take them anyway. I can always give them back if you're right."

She jumped down on to the sand, grabbed

the paintbrushes and stuffed them into her school bag. Antonia was surprised by her friend's behaviour. Sophie was mad about art and her dad was a professional artist. Surely she had enough paintbrushes at home? Then Antonia noticed a bucket abandoned on the sand. It was full of sea water that glistened with an oily sheen. Remembering the news report on television Antonia squeaked in alarm. What about her dolphins? Did Spirit know about the shipwreck? Had he taken his pod far enough out to sea to avoid the oil? The thought of her beautiful friends struggling to breathe, their soft skin covered in sticky black tar, was too much. Protectively she clasped her silver dolphin necklace. "Please keep my dolphins safe," she whispered. The dolphin charm quivered slightly in her hand. Antonia stared at it. Was Spirit about to call her? She waited, her fingers lightly clasping the charm's soft body, but it didn't move again. Disappointment, like sour milk, stuck in her throat and suddenly Antonia wanted to get away from the madness on the beach.

"Hurry up, Sophie," she called. "We're going to be late for school."

Chapter Three

When she arrived at school Antonia sought out Cai, her newest friend. Cai started at Sandy Bay Primary two weeks ago. He was staying with his great-aunt Claudia for six months while his parents worked abroad.

"What's happening at Sea Watch?" she asked. "Is Claudia very busy?"

"Aunty Claudia took in ten oiled birds, all guillemots," said Cai. "I asked if I could stay home to help her clean them, but she wouldn't hear of it. She said there'd still be plenty to do after school. She's hoping you'll come and help too."

"Try keeping me away," said Antonia.

Sophie raised her eyebrows. "Sea Watch-mad, both of you," she groaned, but she was smiling.

Morning lessons went on for ever. Antonia was more concerned about the oil spill in Sandy Bay than how to multiply fractions and she got told off by Miss Brown for not paying attention. It didn't help that lots of her class arrived late because they'd been down to the beach with their parents to see the *Princess*

Romana. Lauren turned up just before lunch and shot Antonia a poisonous look as she took her seat.

"What's with her?" whispered Sophie, who'd been allowed to sit next to Antonia for paired reading.

Antonia shrugged. It was no secret that the two girls disliked each other. When everyone lined up for lunch Lauren shoved Antonia, making her fall against Cai and Toby.

"Slow down, Antonia," Miss Brown sighed. "If you weren't always in such a hurry you wouldn't keep bumping into people."

"It wasn't my fault!" said Antonia indignantly, but Miss Brown had moved on.

"Loser," hissed Lauren.

Taking a deep breath Antonia ignored the

comment. Even though it was difficult, she'd found that not reacting was the best way to deal with Lauren. Afternoon lessons went a little quicker and finally the bell rang for home time.

"Sure you don't want to come to Sea Watch?" Antonia asked Sophie as they stacked their chairs in the corner of the classroom.

Sophie shook her head. "What, to get pecked and pooped on by frightened birds covered in oil? No, thanks. You go enjoy yourself. I'm going to paint a picture of the beach."

In the cloakroom Lauren tried to barge Antonia again, but she smartly sidestepped so the bigger girl fell against the coat pegs and scraped her arm.

"I'll get you for that," Lauren bellowed as Antonia made for the door.

"Just let her try," muttered Cai. "I'll sort her out if she does."

"Thanks, but I can handle her. She doesn't scare me," said Antonia lightly.

"I don't like Lauren. She's a bully." Cai ran a hand through his dark curls. "Aunty Claudia doesn't like bullies either. She's says deep down they're all cowards."

"Your aunt's so cool."

"I know. She's not like a normal aunty, is she? I swear she talks to animals. You should have seen her with this guillemot this morning. They were practically having a conversation."

Antonia laughed. "There is something very special about Claudia," she admitted. "I can't wait to help her with the birds. I hope they're not too badly oiled."

Claudia was looking slightly frazzled when they arrived at Sea Watch. Her clothes were smeared with oil and her curly brown hair was wilder than usual.

"We've been working flat out," she said, pointing to the sink where two ladies wearing thick rubber gloves and disposable plastic aprons were bathing a guillemot. "We've cleaned nineteen birds and the coastguard just brought four more in."

"Tell us what to do and we'll help," said Antonia.

"Well, the oil doesn't just mess up the birds' feathers, it's also poisonous when swallowed. First the birds need their stomachs cleansed with a special solution. I'll do that, you and Cai can take over from Sally and Tess who are on the second stage, cleaning feathers. They're using a special type of washing-up liquid. It's not perfumed. Squeeze a blob on to your hands, then rub it on the bird. Talk to it as you bathe it. Remember a soothing voice can work wonders when an animal is frightened. Rinse the washing-up liquid away with clean water, then put the bird in one of the pens in the back room to dry. The gloves and aprons are in that cupboard."

Antonia and Cai went to the cupboard.

"There's room for both of us in this," laughed Antonia, holding up a plastic apron.

"Tie it round you twice," said Claudia. "You'll have to manage with the gloves.

Everything came in one-size only."

"Jumbo," chuckled Cai, pulling on gloves.

Sea Watch was beginning to fill up with regular volunteers. Antonia waved at Karen and Eleanor, two Year Six girls, also from Sandy Bay Primary.

"Isn't it awful?" called Eleanor. "The coastguard told my dad it was only a minor oil spill. I dread to think of the damage a major one would cause."

The girls disappeared into the back room to clean out the bird pens.

Claudia came over carrying a bedraggled guillemot, its feathers glued together with tarry black oil. "Be careful with this one. He's a wriggler," she said.

Antonia and Cai took their place at the sink.

"Good luck," said Sally, snapping off her rubber gloves. "It's hard messy work. We're exhausted, aren't we, Tess?"

Cai held the bird still while Antonia squeezed a gooey blob of washing-up liquid on to her hands.

"Steady, boy," she murmured.

At first the bird struggled ferociously, snapping his mouth open as he tried to fight everyone off. Cai held him firmly while Antonia worked the washing-up liquid into his sticky black feathers, talking to him in a low soothing voice.

"Poor thing! You're in a bad way. You might need a second wash."

The bird cocked his head and fixed his beady eyes on Antonia. Gradually he stopped wriggling. His breathing slowed as he relaxed until finally he was so still it looked like he'd fallen asleep.

Cai stared at Antonia, his brown eyes astonished.

"What?" Antonia pushed her hair over her shoulder with the back of a gloved hand.

Cai shook his head. "You," he said with a note of wonder. "Look how you calmed the bird. You're so like Aunty Claudia with animals. It's weird."

Antonia blushed. "You are too," she said defensively. "Animals listen when you talk to them."

Cai shrugged, but he looked pleased.

The sink of water was black by the time Antonia had finished washing the guillemot. It made her wonder how badly polluted the sea was. She hoped Spirit had taken Bubbles, Dream, Star and the rest of his pod far away from the ship. A sudden burst of panic gripped her. Did Spirit know about the wreck and the oil leak? What if he brought the pod back too soon? In her mind she saw Bubbles fighting for breath, his blowhole and beautiful silver skin coated in tar. She closed her eyes, forcing the picture to disappear. Panicking wasn't going to help the dolphins. She had to do something practical, like swim out and warn Spirit that it wasn't safe to come back yet. But could she do that? Antonia didn't know whether she could become a Silver Dolphin just because she wanted to. She'd always become one after hearing Spirit's call. Once she'd finished rinsing the soap from the guillemot's feathers she'd go and talk to Claudia. She'd been a Silver Dolphin once so she'd know.

Pulling the plug on the dirty water she waited impatiently for it to drain away.

Chapter Four

It was always hard to get Claudia alone at Sea Watch and today was no exception. A small group of volunteers stuck closely to her, watching how she dealt with the newly admitted birds and asking hundreds of questions. It was late afternoon by the time all the birds had been bathed and left to dry in the small back room. Most of the volunteers went home after that, leaving Claudia to make notes on the treatments given. Antonia helped Cai to clear up the mess in the sink, then, as he went outside to hang the aprons out to dry, she hot-footed it over to Claudia's desk.

"Is everything all right?" asked Claudia.

Before Antonia had a chance to reply, Cai came back.

"Yes, I just came to say..." Antonia hesitated. She desperately wanted to ask Claudia if she could become a Silver Dolphin without waiting for the dolphin's call, so she could warn Spirit about the oil spill. But she couldn't ask when Cai was hovering.

"Is there anything else that needs doing?" she finished lamely.

Antonia wasn't surprised at the look Cai gave her. It was a silly question. There was always something to do at Sea Watch. Claudia must have thought the same, but she didn't laugh. She took Antonia's hand and stared deeply into her grey-green eyes. Antonia caught her breath. She wanted to blink, but her eyes stayed firmly open as if she was caught in a spotlight. She felt slightly dizzy, as though Claudia was tapping directly into her thoughts.

"You know what needs doing," Claudia whispered.

"But can I..." Antonia hesitated, aware of the open curiosity on Cai's face.

You'll have to work that out for yourself.

Antonia jumped. Claudia had remained silent yet she could hear her voice in her head

as clearly as if she'd spoken aloud. Had she
imagined it?

Go work it out.

Claudia smiled knowingly, then dropped
Antonia's hand.

Silver Dolphin.

Claudia kept smiling and suddenly Antonia
realised she had her answer. She was the Silver
Dolphin. It was up to her to work this problem
out for herself.

"Home time," said Claudia. "See you
tomorrow?"

"Yes," said Antonia, feeling happier. "Definitely."

Hurriedly she said goodbye to Cai. As she
ran down Claudia's road Antonia calculated
she had an hour before Mum would expect her
home for tea. She headed towards the beach.

Minutes later she was there and Sandy Bay was in full view. Eyes widening in surprise, Antonia stopped to stare. The beach was heaving with people. Not tourists building sandcastles or lying in the sun, these people were scavenging. Armed with bags the size of sacks they were raiding the beach like hungry ants in a larder. Several people had waded out to sea where wooden crates were still floating ashore. One man wore a wetsuit. Two police officers stood on the stone pier watching the events as if they could hardly believe what was happening.

Antonia was shocked. She hadn't expected this. She thought the *Princess Romana* would have been fixed by now and sailed away, leaving behind only the damage caused by the oil spill. But the boat was slumped against the horizon looking like one of the bedraggled birds that had come into Sea Watch.

With a frustrated sigh, Antonia dropped down on to the beach and weaving her way through the crowds made for the rocky arm where the bay ended. There were people on the rocks too and Antonia had to scramble further round than she wanted to before she left everyone behind. She kicked off her sandals, peeled off her ankle socks and wedged them under her school bag. Gingerly she made her way across the slippery barnacle-encrusted rocks to the sea. The water was cool and it made her hot feet tingle. Antonia stood for a moment trying to quell the nervous butterflies dancing in her stomach.

What would happen when she waded further into the sea? Would her legs meld together so she could swim like a dolphin or would she just end up with a soaking wet dress? There was only one way to find out. Antonia took a step forward and then another. Nothing happened and Antonia felt a rush of disappointment. Now what? She was a good swimmer, but there was no way she could swim out and find Spirit unless she became a Silver Dolphin.

"But I am the Silver Dolphin," she said aloud.

Antonia fingered the dolphin charm hanging round her neck. When Claudia had explained Silver Dolphins to her she'd said that for the magic to happen she had to believe in it.

"So believe it," she told herself.

"I am a Silver Dolphin. I am a Silver Dolphin."

Antonia whispered the words, knowing they were true.

She continued to wade out into the sea until the water reached her chest, then plunging forward, she swam. Immediately her legs melded together, flicking at the water like a dolphin's tail. Antonia's cheer came out as a whistle. The magic had worked! Antonia was so excited she began to porpoise, leaping in and out of the water as she swam. A long while later she slowed down, then stopped to tread water using her legs like a tail to keep her afloat. She'd swum a long way. She couldn't see Sandy Bay beach and even the *Princess Romana*

was a tiny dot in the distance. Antonia was bursting with happiness. Discovering she could be a Silver Dolphin when she wanted to was amazing. She couldn't wait to share her news with Bubbles. But how was she going to find her dolphin friend?

The sea stretched away from her in a vast expanse of blue that went on for ever. If she wasn't careful she could get so lost that she might never find her way home. Squashing her rising panic Antonia realised there was a way to find her dolphin friends. Opening her mouth wide she called out to them in dolphin clicks and squeaks.

Chapter Five

At first there was no reply. Treading water, Antonia listened to the sound of the sea filling her ears like the breath of an enormous sleeping beast. Occasionally a wave smacked against her, but apart from the sea sounds there was nothing else to hear. Antonia scanned the horizon, unsure whether to swim on or to give up and go home. Then suddenly her body began to tingle. At once Antonia recognised the sensation. It was caused by vibrations in the water. Was something coming her way? The vibrations grew stronger and then turned into a welcome clicking sound.

"Spirit," she called.

"Silver Dolphin?" Spirit sounded incredulous. "Is that you?"

"Yes," clicked Antonia, excitement making her squeak. "Where are you?"

"Not far. Stay where you are. I'll come to you."

Spirit's voice was serious and Antonia felt a pang of uncertainty. Was he annoyed because she had come without being called? As she waited Antonia's stomach churned uncomfortably.

A while later Antonia felt more vibrations in the sea. These were stronger, pinging against her skin like hailstones. She scanned the sea's surface and at last she saw two dolphins, their bodies making silver arches as they leapt in and out of the water. As they drew closer Antonia recognised the bigger dolphin as Spirit. The smaller one was almost identical except that the blaze across his flank was more amber than yellow.

"Bubbles!"

Antonia hadn't realised she'd been holding her breath until it came out in a sudden rush of air. Spirit couldn't be angry with her if he'd brought Bubbles along. Antonia longed to swim to meet Bubbles, but held back, remembering why she was here. Bubbles also recognised the importance of the occasion and slowed, letting Spirit greet Antonia first. Spirit swam right up to Antonia, his liquid eyes holding hers as he gently rubbed her, nose to nose.

"Silver Dolphin!" he exclaimed. "What brings you here? Did another dolphin call you?"

"There's been an oil leak from a ship that ran aground in the storm. I came to warn you to stay out at sea. It's not safe for you to come inshore until the oil has broken up."

"You mean you came on your own to warn us of the danger? No other dolphin called you?"

Antonia nodded.

A strange expression crossed Spirit's face, then he lightly touched the top of Antonia's head with his flipper.

"I knew it," he whispered. "Yours is a very powerful gift, Silver Dolphin. Use it wisely."

Antonia flushed. What did Spirit mean by that? She was going to ask, but Spirit moved back to include Bubbles in the conversation and the moment passed.

"Thank you, Silver Dolphin. That was a brave thing to do. We'll definitely stay out at sea until the oil has broken up."

Bubbles made a sad face, then nudged his father in the side.

"Dad, it might be ages before I see the Silver Dolphin again. Please can we play for a bit?"

Spirit clicked a laugh.

"Swim along, my little dolphin. Go have fun with your friend."

"Bubbly!" whistled Bubbles. "Let's play

seaweed tag. The first one to find some seaweed's *not* it."

He dived down towards the seabed, but Spirit blocked Antonia from following with his tail.

"You've come a long way. Can you find your way back?" he asked.

Antonia looked towards the *Princess Romana*, a small black dot on the flat blue sea.

"Yes, home is that way."

"Call me if you get lost," said Spirit.

"Thank you," said Antonia.

A fountain of water spouted up behind them as Bubbles surfaced.

"You're it," he whistled, tossing a strand of seaweed at Antonia, but missing. "Whoops, sorry, Dad."

Spirit shook the seaweed off his head and threw it back at Bubbles.

"I should ground you for that," he said.

"Aw, Dad! You wouldn't!"

"Hmmm," said Spirit, a twinkle in his eye. "Better swim along before I do."

"Come on, Flipper Feet." Bubbles flicked the seaweed at Antonia. "Catch me if you can."

Antonia hesitated, then Spirit reached out and gently rubbed his nose against hers. Self-consciously Antonia rubbed Spirit's nose back.

"Be safe, Silver Dolphin," he clicked, then he sped off, dipping and diving through the water.

Immediately Antonia went after Bubbles with the seaweed trailing from her fingers in a long green ribbon. The water was clear and

Antonia had no trouble finding her friend. She raced after him, but just as she was almost close enough to tag him, Bubbles dived deeper.

"Missed," he chuckled.

Antonia swam faster, her legs furiously kicking the water. This wasn't like playing tag inshore. There was no shallow seabed with rocks to hide behind, just acres of blue-green water with the occasional strand of seaweed floating by. With a neat somersault Bubbles changed direction, but guessing he would do something like that, Antonia was ready and somersaulted too. The gap closed and stretching out her hand Antonia looped the seaweed over Bubbles's tail.

"Got you," she called. "You're it now."

They played for ages, leaping out of the sea

then diving deep, draping the seaweed over each other until it was battered and torn into a tissue-thin strip. Finally Antonia speared the seaweed on Bubbles's fin.

"Game over," she panted. "I really must go home."

"I'll swim some of the way with you," said Bubbles.

"No way," said Antonia. "There's oil, remember."

Bubbles made a sad face.

"I might not see you for ages."

"But I'll be thinking of you," said Antonia.

"And I'll think of you back," Bubbles clicked.

They rubbed noses several times before Antonia pulled away.

"See you soon," she whistled.

"You too, Silver Dolphin," clicked Bubbles.

It was a long swim back, but Antonia was too happy to notice. Spirit had been amazed to see her so far out at sea. He'd said she was very powerful. She swam faster, conscious that she mustn't be late home. Mum was very strict about knowing where Antonia was and what time she would be back; she would be grounded for being late. As Antonia neared the shore her heart sank. If anything, the beach was more crowded than before. The man in the wetsuit had been joined by someone else and two speedboats were circling at the mouth of the bay. Quickly Antonia dived underwater, hoping that everyone would be too busy scavenging to notice her swimming ashore. She kept going until her knees bumped on the seabed and then she surfaced. A wave splashed in her face. It tasted bad and made her cough. Antonia waded through the surf, her legs working separately where seconds before they had felt joined together. The water poured off, leaving her school dress as dry as if she'd been basking in the sun. Antonia scrambled over the rocks to claim her things. Her bag was where she'd left it; luckily no scavengers had found it. Smoothing down her yellow-checked school dress Antonia noticed several dark streaks on her front. She rubbed one with her finger. It smelt like the bad taste in her mouth as she came ashore. It was oil! Shocked, Antonia picked at it with her fingernail, but it didn't make any difference. The stains were there to stay. Pulling on her shoes and socks Antonia knew she should be upset about spoiling her dress, but all she could feel was relief. Thank goodness she'd found Spirit and warned him to stay away from the shore. Messing up her dress was a small price to pay for protecting her friends.

Chapter Six

ntonia arrived home at the same time as Dad came back from working at the garage he owned. She waited while he parked his car and they went indoors together. Mum was preparing the evening meal while Jessica sat at the kitchen table, glued to the television. Antonia wasn't surprised to see Sandy Bay on the news again. There had to be something special on for her mother to allow television at tea time. She was surprised, however, to find that Sandy Bay had made it on to the national news.

"People have been arriving in Sandy Bay all day," the newsreader gushed. "The police are urging scavengers to hand in property recovered from the beach so that it can be returned to its rightful owners."

"Vultures, the lot of them!" said Dad, squeezing past his wife to wash his hands at the sink. "It's nothing more than common theft. I had a girl come in today with her older brother. Lauren something; she claimed she was a friend of yours, Antonia. She had a huge sack of car bits she'd found on the beach. Her brother asked me to buy them and turned nasty when I told him I wouldn't."

"Lauren Hampton," said Antonia, suddenly realising why Lauren had been particularly mean to her at school. "She's no friend of mine."

"I'm glad to hear it," said Dad as he turned round to reach for the towel. "I won't have any of my family behaving like that. I don't know what's got into people. It's—" Dad broke off as he noticed Antonia's dress. "Whatever have you done to yourself?"

Antonia blushed so fiercely even her scalp turned red. She'd completely forgotten about her dress. "It's oil," she said.

"Antonia!" Mum stopped arranging cucumber slices around a dish of salad to study her daughter's clothes. "Were you on the beach today?"

For a split second Antonia considered telling her parents she'd got oil on her clothes helping out at Sea Watch, but she couldn't do it. She felt guilty enough about all the fibs she'd had to tell to cover up for being a Silver Dolphin.

She nodded. "Yes, I was."

"And you didn't take me. That's so mean," wailed Jessica.

Dad's eyes narrowed to slits. "What were you doing on the beach?"

Antonia shrugged. "I only wanted to have a look. Nothing like this has happened before. Everyone's talking about it at school."

"So long as looking is all you were doing. If I find you've been taking things from the beach, young lady, you'll be grounded for ever. Do you hear me?"

"Mark," Antonia's mum put a hand on her husband's arm. "She knows not to take other people's things, don't you, darling?"

"Of course I do," said Antonia.

"Good. Promise me you'll stay away from the beach. I don't want you anywhere near it until this circus is over." Dad looked at Antonia sternly.

"I promise." Antonia wasn't quite able to meet her dad's eye as, under her breath, she added, "Unless Spirit calls me."

After tea, to ease her conscience, Antonia stacked the dishwasher, took the recycling out and emptied the vegetable waste into the composter. Composting was her least favourite job. She hated the writhing knot of worms that clung to the underside of the lid each time the composting bin was opened.

"Yuk!" she exclaimed as several blood-red worms fell and almost landed on her bare feet.

Replacing the lid Antonia stood in the garden staring out at the bay. She hoped the oil would disperse quickly. She also hoped that the growing number of speedboats would go away and leave the bay in peace. Antonia longed to return to the sea and swim with Bubbles.

At bedtime she was sure she wouldn't sleep, but to her surprise she dropped off immediately, sleeping soundly until the alarm woke her.

It was Sophie who looked like she'd hardly slept. When Antonia called for her friend on the way to school Sophie's eyes were ringed with shadows and she couldn't stop yawning. She didn't talk much, but Antonia was too wrapped up in her own thoughts to wonder about it. Her stomach bubbled with excitement each time she remembered how she'd become a Silver Dolphin on her own. She wished she could share her secret with someone apart from Claudia, but she knew she mustn't. What if the magic stopped working because she'd talked about it? Turning her thoughts to Sea Watch, Antonia wondered how the injured seabirds were this morning. She would ask Cai as soon as she got to school. Halfway down Sandy Bay Road

Sophie suddenly asked, "Can we go to the beach?"

"Sorry, but I can't," said Antonia. "I promised Dad I'd keep away."

"It'll only take a minute. Please, Antonia." Sophie twisted a brown strand of hair around her finger. "I've got to take these paintbrushes back. I found out that it's stealing to keep things that have fallen from a boat. Mum and Dad would be really upset if they knew what I did. I hardly slept last night thinking about it."

"I told you it was stealing yesterday!"

"I know." Sophie was embarrassed. "I thought you were wrong."

Antonia didn't want to make Sophie go to the beach alone, but she wished she didn't have to break her promise to Dad.

"Oh, all right," she said. "But we need to be quick. If we're late for school we'll have to sign in at the office and then I'll be in trouble."

Antonia's mum worked in the office at Sandy Bay Primary School. Most of the time it was nice having Mum around, but it also had its disadvantages.

School bags bumping on their backs, the girls jogged towards the beach. As they grew nearer, the pavement became more crowded and Antonia kept hold of Sophie's hand so they didn't get separated by the wave of people heading towards the sand. At the promenade they stopped for Sophie to get the paintbrushes out of her school bag.

"Wait here," said Sophie, "I won't be long."

"No." Antonia made a lightning decision. "I'm coming with you. There are too many people around. If we separate we might lose each other."

"Are you sure?"

"Yes."

Antonia couldn't risk losing Sophie. That would surely make them late for school. Antonia hated disobeying Dad, but it wasn't like she was doing anything wrong. She was helping her friend to put something right and Sophie would have done the same for her if the situation had been reversed. Trying not to think about her promise, Antonia forced her way on to the sand.

Sophie glanced around anxiously. "Shall I

hand them to a policeman or just drop them somewhere?"

"I can't see any police," said Antonia. "It's too crowded."

"Here then," said Sophie, dropping the paintbrushes as if they had suddenly become too hot to hold.

"They might get trodden on there." Antonia stooped and picked them up. "Let's leave them on top of that litter bin where they can be seen."

She squeezed her way over to the bin, picking her way round a lawn mower and a set of golf clubs, and left the paintbrushes on its lid.

"Right, let's go."

"Hang on." Sophie screwed her eyes up. "I

think there's some of our class over there by the lifeguard's chair."

"All the more reason to get going." Antonia spun Sophie round and pushed her back towards the promenade. "We're not supposed to be down here, remember?"

"Ooh! I forgot!" exclaimed Sophie, turning red.

They squeezed their way across the crowded beach, not daring to look back until they were safely on the promenade. By then the Sandy Bay school children had been swallowed up in the crowd. Antonia was relieved. That had been close, but she didn't think they'd been spotted.

"Come on," she said, breaking into a jog. "I need to find Cai before lessons start. I want to know how the birds at Sea Watch are doing."

Sophie grinned.

"You and your animals! Come on then, we'll run."

Chapter Seven

There was no sign of Cai in the school playground. Disappointed, Antonia wandered into the classroom and sat down. She kept her eyes on the door as the classroom slowly began to fill up. Lauren and Becky came in together, talking loudly. Lauren seemed excited. Her eyes swept the room and seeing

Antonia, a cruel smile played on her lips. Antonia's heart dipped as Lauren ambled towards her. What did the big girl want?

"Your dad's a bit choosy, isn't he? He wouldn't buy stuff from my brother yesterday."

Antonia shrugged and picking up a pencil, she began to doodle in her work book.

"Does your dad know you took stuff from the beach too?"

Antonia's heart thudded loudly. So she had been seen this morning. Carefully she turned her doodling into a tiny dolphin leaping a wave.

"Don't know what you're talking about," she said quietly.

"Paintbrushes," Lauren grinned nastily. "We saw you this morning, didn't we, Becks?"

Becky nodded vigorously.

"Then you'd have seen I was putting the paintbrushes somewhere safe," said Antonia coldly. "I left them on a bin where they wouldn't get broken."

Lauren narrowed her eyes. "Maybe we didn't see that bit. Did you see her leave them on the bin, Becky?"

"No, I don't remember seeing that," Becky sniggered.

Antonia shrugged as if she wasn't interested, but her heart was banging even faster. "That's your problem."

"No, it's not!" Lauren squatted down so her face was millimetres from Antonia's. "It's yours. I might just mention it to your mum. See what she says."

"Mum doesn't listen to tell-tales," said Antonia calmly while inside she was bubbling with panic. Antonia knew Mum would believe her version of events, but she might ground her for breaking her promise to stay off the beach. That would mean no Sea Watch and worse still there would be no going out to answer Spirit's call.

"'Mum doesn't listen to tell-tales'," mimicked Lauren. "Well, you won't mind me telling her then, will you?" She barged Antonia's chair, then walked away laughing.

"Is everything OK?" Cai came into the classroom and hurried over, his dark eyes full of concern. "Is Lauren being a pain?"

Antonia was angry and scared, but she wasn't going to let on. If she acted like she didn't care maybe Lauren would give up and annoy someone else instead.

"It's nothing. How's things at Sea Watch?"

Cai studied her for a moment with his face creased into a frown. Then he said, "We only had three new birds in this morning. According to the coastguard the oil's breaking up much faster than everyone thought it would."

"Good," said Antonia. "That means..." She was about to say that Spirit and his pod could come back soon, but stopped herself in time.

"What?" prompted Cai.

"It means less damage to the sea," Antonia said lamely. "How are the birds that came in yesterday?"

Cai paused. "Eight of them died last night, including the ones we bathed."

Antonia felt as if a hole had opened up in her stomach. First Lauren and now this! She swallowed, forcing herself not to get upset.

"What happened? Did we do something wrong?"

Cai shook his head. "It wasn't anyone's fault. Aunty Claudia said it's quite common for birds to die after they've been cleaned up. Some have been too badly poisoned to recover and some just die from shock."

Miss Brown came in carrying the register so Cai went to his place. Antonia stared out of the window wishing school was over and she could go to Sea Watch. Lessons seemed a waste of time when she could be helping there instead. She was also longing to tell Claudia that she'd been to see Spirit. Antonia was almost certain she hadn't been imagining things yesterday when she'd heard Claudia's voice in her head, telling her to work things out for herself.

"Antonia Lee, are you here or am I looking at a cardboard cut-out?" Miss Brown's voice broke into Antonia's thoughts, bringing her out of her daydream.

"Here, Miss," she answered meekly.

"Nice to have you with us." Miss Brown's pen flicked down the register as she continued calling out names. When she'd finished she held the register up in front of her.

"Who'll take this to the office for me?"

"Me." Lauren shot Antonia a sly grin. "I'll go and give it to Mrs Lee."

Antonia pretended to flick through her work

book while inside her heart was thumping again. If Miss Brown picked Lauren, then she was done for.

"Lauren, don't call out. Luke, your hand's up. You can do it."

Antonia's breath hissed out with relief. Then realising it was going to be a nightmare if she had to worry about Lauren telling on her all day, she had a brainwave. She would go and confess to Mum herself; far better to be grounded for owning up than because she'd been snitched on by Lauren. Antonia could barely concentrate during maths and at playtime she was first out of the classroom. She ran all the way to the office.

"Walk," bellowed Mr Cordier, the head teacher, coming out of his room. "Oh, it's you

Antonia. Funny, I thought a herd of buffalo was travelling past."

Giggling, Antonia slowed to a fast walk. She was nervous about telling Mum she'd broken her promise, but at the same time she was keen to get it over with. There was a queue at the office. Antonia waited impatiently, hopping from foot to foot and when her turn came she was so anxious her tongue tripped over her words. To her enormous relief Mum wasn't cross.

"Because you were helping a friend *and* you owned up. But please don't disobey me or Dad again," she added.

Antonia could hardly look at Mum. If Spirit called then she would be forced to disobey both her parents.

"Cheer up," said Mum, mistaking her crestfallen look. "It's not like you'll be missing anything. The police are temporarily closing all the beaches in the area to stop the looting. I heard it on the news before Jessica and I left this morning. Extra police are being drafted in to keep people away. Anyone found on a local beach will be prosecuted."

"Prosecuted?" Antonia's insides turned to ice.

"Taken to court," said Mum. "Run along now. I'm too busy to stand here chatting to you all day."

Pulling herself together Antonia went outside. She spent the last few minutes of playtime making it up to Sophie, who was not pleased that Antonia had disappeared without saying where she was going and even less pleased that she'd told her mum about the paintbrushes.

"That means I'll have to tell my mum now, just in case your mum mentions it," Sophie complained.

"Your mum will be fine," said Antonia automatically. "You'll feel much better once you've told the truth."

"Then why don't you feel better?" asked Sophie grumpily. "You're as white as a ghost."

"I've got a headache," said Antonia, rubbing her forehead. What if Spirit called her now? How on earth would she answer his call with police everywhere and all the beaches closed? Crossing her fingers tightly Antonia hoped that Spirit wouldn't need her help.

Chapter Eight

Cai and Antonia were on their way to Sea Watch. Cai was telling Antonia about his surfing lesson the weekend before.

"Then I fell off the surfboard, washed up on the beach and landed next to a lady who screamed and dropped her ice cream on her husband," Cai chuckled.

"That is so funny," Antonia giggled. "Are you going to try surfing again? It's brilliant fun once you get the hang of it."

"Course I'm going to try again," said Cai. "I don't give up that easily. You'd better watch out. It won't be long before I'm as good as you."

"Then we can surf together," said Antonia enthusiastically. Surfing with Cai would be brilliant. He was great fun to be with. "Only we can't surf now the beaches are closed."

"That won't be for long," said Cai. "There can't be much more stuff to come ashore. Who's that on Aunty Claudia's drive? He doesn't look very happy."

A middle-aged man with balding hair and a paunch was climbing into a green car. His face was like a thundercloud. He slammed the door and snapped on his seat belt. As Antonia stared at the man a feeling of unease came over her. It made her skin prickle with goose bumps. The car engine roared to life and the man took off, his wheels spinning gravel into the flowerbed. Cai broke into a run and Antonia followed him into the back garden. Side by side they raced down the sloping lawn towards the large wooden building at the bottom. Suddenly, the door opened and Claudia came out, her lips pressed together in a firm line. Antonia had never seen her look so angry before and she felt a little scared.

"What's the matter?" panted Cai. "Who was that man? What did he want?"

Claudia's nostrils flared as she struggled to control her anger.

"He came from the city," she said at last. "He's bought a motorboat and he wanted to launch it from my beach."

"I thought all the beaches were closed," said Antonia.

"Not the beach at the end of my garden. The police can't close that as it belongs to me," said Claudia. "As you know it's only a small area. That man wanted to use my beach as a base to scavenge from. He offered me a percentage of anything he found and got very nasty when I turned his offer down."

"Are you all right?" Antonia touched Claudia on the arm. "Shall I make you a cup of tea?" There was a kettle in the Sea Watch building.

Antonia's mum always made a cup of tea when there was a crisis. Antonia wasn't sure why, but Mum seemed to think it helped.

Claudia smiled. "No, thank you. One of you could go and close the gates for me, though. I leave them open for my adult volunteers who drive here, but I think I'd better keep them shut to deter any more strangers from coming in."

"Let's chain them together with a huge padlock. That'll keep people out," said Cai.

"I don't think we need to go that far." Claudia smiled at him. "I don't want to keep everyone away. Come and find me on the beach when you're done. You can help me to take some sea samples. I've been checking for oil, but we seem to be all right so far. The oil hasn't reached our beach."

Claudia strode towards the beach and Cai raced back up the garden to close the gates. Antonia stayed rooted to the spot, relief flooding through her. She could hardly believe her good luck. She hadn't realised Claudia owned her patch of beach. So she could swim out to Spirit if he called her. Then a new thought struck her and Antonia's mouth widened into a huge smile. Why wait for Spirit to call? She would go and visit the dolphins again, as she'd done yesterday. Only this time, purely for fun. She knew Bubbles would be pleased to see her and maybe she could persuade Dream to play with them too. Antonia really wanted to make friends with Bubbles's big sister.

"What are you grinning at? You look like

you've had some really good news." Cai was back from shutting the gates.

"Nothing, I mean it's just I love being at Sea Watch," Antonia blustered. "It's much more fun than school."

"Lauren's not getting to you, is she?" asked Cai, his brown eyes narrowing.

"Nothing I can't handle," said Antonia lightly. "Come on. Let's go and help Claudia to collect samples of sea water."

There was so much to do at Sea Watch. After collecting the sea water they gave a second bath to three birds who'd been very badly oiled, and then cleaned out the pens of the recovering birds. The time sped past. With a start Antonia realised she didn't have time for a private chat with Claudia if she wanted to see Bubbles before she had to go to her swimming club. Quickly she finished topping up water bowls, then washed her hands in the sink.

"See you tomorrow," she said to Cai as she shook her hands dry.

Cai raised his eyebrows. "You're going early."

"Swimming club," said Antonia, her eyes searching the room for Claudia. "I've been moved to the Wednesday class. Can you say goodbye to Claudia for me?"

"Sure," said Cai. "See you tomorrow."

Antonia checked the garden was empty before heading down to the beach. Inside she was bubbling with excitement. She couldn't wait to see Bubbles's face when she turned up again. She knew he'd be pleased and surprised to see her. Claudia's boat was tied to the wooden gate that opened on to the beach. Sitting on the sand Antonia pulled off her shoes and socks, then tucked them inside the boat. She felt far more confident than she had yesterday and was sure that she would find her dolphins again. She could almost feel the magic fizzing round her body. Taking a slow calming breath Antonia imagined herself swimming in the sea.

"I am a Silver Dolphin," she said, walking into the surf.

The water reached her stomach and she was about to start swimming when a cry stopped her.

"Antonia!"

97

Surprised, she spun round. The afternoon sun dazzled her eyes, but there was no mistaking Claudia's tall figure running down the beach.

"Antonia, wait!"

Chapter Nine

laudia stopped at the edge of the surf, her face wrinkled with concern. "What are you doing?" she asked.

"I... I... I'm going to find Spirit," Antonia stuttered.

"Why? He didn't call for you." Claudia's fingers went to her throat and she pulled a silver dolphin necklace from under her shirt. "I may be too old to swim and help the dolphins, but I still like to know what's going on," she said wistfully.

Antonia was pleased that Claudia was still in touch with the dolphins.

"I've got something really exciting to tell you," she burst out. "I can become a Silver Dolphin whenever I want. Yesterday I swam out to sea to warn Spirit about the oil."

Antonia thought Claudia would be thrilled by her news, but she didn't look it. Instead she asked, "So why are you going to find him today?"

Feeling uncertain, Antonia twiddled with her own dolphin charm. "I wanted to swim with Bubbles," she said at last.

"I think," said Claudia gently, "it's time we had a little chat."

As Antonia splashed out of the sea she was shocked to find that the skirt of her dress was soaking wet.

"What happened?" she asked. "Why isn't the magic working?"

"Because you weren't needed," said Claudia. "You can only become a Silver Dolphin if there is work to do."

She led Antonia up the beach and sat her down by the Sea Watch boat.

"Being a Silver Dolphin is a very big responsibility," Claudia began. "And for you there is more. Do you remember me telling you that we share the same birthday?"

"Midsummer's Day," said Antonia. Claudia

had told her that the night she'd first explained Silver Dolphins to her.

Claudia nodded. "A Silver Dolphin who is born on the longest day of the year is even more powerful. You'll find, as you learn to use your magic, that there are lots of things you can do that other Silver Dolphins can't."

"Like becoming a Silver Dolphin when I want to?" Antonia asked.

"That's right. But with great power comes an even greater responsibility. You must use your magic wisely. You must never interfere with nature unless you are putting right a wrong caused by humans. And you may only become a Silver Dolphin when you are needed. You can't become one just for fun."

Hot shame flooded through Antonia. She

stared at her feet, but Claudia put a finger under her chin and gently lifted her face up.

"Don't be too hard on yourself. You're doing a great job. You've learnt so much in a very short time."

"Antonia, what happened?"

Cai vaulted over the small gate in the fence separating beach from garden and ran over. "Why is your dress wet?"

His face was full of concern, causing Antonia another twang of guilt, knowing that she'd messed up.

"A little accident," said Claudia smoothly. "I asked Antonia to get one last sea sample for me and she slipped and fell in. Help me up, Cai, there's a good lad."

Claudia held out her hand and Cai, lips

twitching, pulled his great-aunt to her feet.

"Look at you!" Cai started to laugh as Antonia scrambled up. "Your dress is soaked! You can't go home like that, can she, Aunty Claudia? Can she stay for tea while she dries off?"

"I've got swimming club tonight," said Antonia, glad of the excuse. Normally she would have loved to stay for tea, but she couldn't face it right now. She needed time alone to think about what Claudia had told her.

"Come tomorrow then," said Cai. "She can, can't she?"

Claudia nodded. "Antonia's always welcome here. She doesn't need an invitation."

"Thanks, I'd like that," said Antonia.

On the way home Antonia stopped halfway up Sandy Bay Road to look down at the beach. It was still like an enormous jumble sale, staffed by tiny blue figures that had to be the police. The beach was cordoned off with blue and white incident tape that rippled in the sea breeze. A tiny figure sat on the edge of the promenade, sketching away. Sophie. Even at this distance there was no mistaking Antonia's best friend.

I've two best friends now, Antonia decided. *Sophie and Cai.*

She was pleased that Sophie didn't mind her spending time with Cai at Sea Watch.

"Why should I mind?" Sophie had answered when Antonia asked her about it. "Cai goes round with Toby at school so it's not like you keep leaving me out."

Antonia took a last look at the beach. With the stricken *Princess Romana* lying at the mouth of the bay and the lost cargo still littering the beach, Sandy Bay had never looked so full. Yet to Antonia, knowing her dolphins were far out at sea, the place felt empty.

"Please hurry and clear up the mess," Antonia urged the tiny policemen down below as she continued walking home.

Straight after an early tea Antonia put her swimming things in a bag along with Dad's mobile phone. Her swimming teacher had moved her up a group to train with the squad and the session lasted for two hours.

"Don't forget to ring me on the landline when you've finished and I'll come and pick you up," said Mr Lee, jangling his car keys.

"Can I come too?" asked Jessica.

"No, darling," said Mrs Lee. "It's time for your bath."

"Aw!" squeaked Jessica. "Not fair."

"Never mind, Jess, it'll soon be the weekend and your lesson," said Antonia.

The swimming pool was a short drive away. As Mr Lee pulled up outside Antonia had a strange sensation that Spirit needed her. Seconds later her dolphin charm began to tremble.

"I'll watch you run in," said Dad. "Wait inside for me when you've finished. It'll be too late for you to come out on your own."

"OK," said Antonia, only half listening.

Whatever could Spirit want? It must be a

real emergency for him to call her at this time of the evening.

"Spirit, I hear your call," she whispered under her breath as the dolphin charm vibrated more strongly. Antonia climbed out of the car just as the charm began to whistle.

"Have fun," said Dad.

"Thanks," she called, and waved.

Antonia raced inside the swimming-pool building, a plan forming in her head. The lady at the desk smiled at her as she approached.

"Swimming squad?" she asked.

"Er, yes."

"Name?"

"Antonia Lee," said Antonia, trying to ignore the vibrating charm and its high-pitched whistle. "I can't swim tonight. I just came to say that something's come up, but I'll be here next week."

"Thanks for letting us know. I'll pass the message on to your coach," said the lady, picking up her pen.

Gratefully Antonia hurried back outside. Dad had gone home and she had a couple of hours before he was expecting to pick her up. Heading left down the street Antonia ran all the way to Claudia's. She wondered if she should call at the house and ask permission to use Claudia's beach, but decided against it. What if Cai answered the front door? Besides, Claudia would know from her own necklace that Spirit needed help. Antonia stopped a few paces away from Claudia's shut gates to get her breath back. Then quickly she let herself in and crept down the side of the house, keeping to the edge of the garden so the bushes would mask her. The Sea Watch building was locked up for the night. Antonia hurried past it, then hopped across the sand, pulling off her sandals as she went. She left the sandals and her swimming bag inside the Sea Watch boat. The sea was calm, unlike her wildly vibrating dolphin charm. With a sense of foreboding Antonia cupped it in her hand. Something serious must have happened for the charm to react like this. Quickly she splashed further out to sea.

"Spirit, I'm on my way," she whistled as her legs melded together and at last she was swimming like a dolphin.

Chapter Ten

A short way out to sea Antonia heard the hum of a boat and looking round saw a police launch cruising in a circular path. For a second she panicked and treading water, she almost put her hands up in the air like she'd seen people do in films. The launch seemed to be patrolling between Sandy Bay and the

Princess Romana. At this distance Antonia thought she probably couldn't be seen, but she wasn't taking any chances. After a deep breath she plunged under the sea's surface and swam on out of sight. Soon her skin began tingling and Antonia guessed from the strength of the vibrations that a dolphin was approaching. She surfaced and swam on, her body slicing through the sea as she hurried to meet Spirit and find out why he'd called. But as the dolphin shape became visible Antonia drew up in shock.

"Bubbles!" she exclaimed.

Bubbles's eyes were bright with panic and he didn't greet Antonia with his usual exuberance.

"This way, Silver Dolphin," he clicked. "Hurry."

Checking that Antonia was following him Bubbles swam away. Icy fingers of panic clutched Antonia's stomach. Where was Spirit? Was he hurt? Antonia raced after Bubbles, wishing she knew what was wrong. They swam for ages until up ahead Antonia saw shadowy shapes in the water. As she swam closer the shapes became dolphins, almost thirty of them slowly circling in a tightknit ring. Antonia stopped in amazement. As Bubbles approached, two of them parted, allowing Bubbles to swim between them into the ring's centre. Antonia followed, wondering what she would find inside the dolphin circle. Bubbles came to an abrupt halt.

"She's here," he whistled.

"Thank goodness."

Spirit swam forward and nudged Antonia into the centre of the ring where Star, his wife, was anxiously tending a smaller dolphin. Antonia's heart raced at the sight of the blood seeping into the water. Then she realised the injured dolphin was Dream.

"She got hit by a speedboat," choked Bubbles. "Make her better, Silver Dolphin. Please make her better."

"Hush," said Spirit, stroking Bubbles with a flipper. "Don't worry, son. The Silver Dolphin will do what she can."

Antonia stretched out a hand. "It's OK, I won't hurt you," she murmured as Dream flinched.

Antonia tried not to look too worried by the large gash directly above Dream's left flipper, but inside she was panicking about how she could treat it.

"She was out at sea bow-riding behind a boat when a second boat with a blue flashing light came up. The first boat turned unexpectedly and caught Dream side on," said Spirit.

"The boat with the blue light was a police launch," said Antonia, suddenly working it all out. "I expect the other boat was a looter."

As she examined Dream's wound she wondered if the looter was the same person who'd wanted to use Claudia's beach.

Star stroked her daughter's head with a flipper.

"Can you make her better, Silver Dolphin?" she clicked anxiously.

Antonia breathed deeply, trying to hide the panic that was still scrambling her insides. How was she expected to help Dream? She wasn't a vet.

Go work it out.

Antonia blinked. The voice in her head was Claudia's. It gave her confidence. She was a Silver Dolphin. She could work out how to save Dream. Antonia thought about all the times she'd fallen over and cut her own knees. Mum had cleaned the cuts then bandaged them to stop the bleeding. But what could she use as a bandage?

"I need something to stop the blood," she whistled. "Seaweed," she added, finding inspiration. "Bubbles, can you find me lots of seaweed?"

Bubbles leapt into action.

"On it," he whistled, swimming back through the circle of dolphins.

"Bubbles, wait," clicked Spirit. "I'll come with you. Dream's in safe hands now the Silver Dolphin is here."

The responsibility made Antonia shiver. Spirit had such faith in her. Dream was losing a lot of blood. The water around her was an ugly shade of red. There must be something more she could do. Gently Antonia pressed the sides of the wound together with her hands. Dream winced and shyly Antonia clicked soothing noises. She felt awkward touching the dolphin. She'd been longing to get to know her better, but not like this!

"Does it hurt?" clicked Star anxiously as Dream winced again.

"I'm fine," said Dream, through gritted teeth.

"What's bow-riding?" asked Antonia, hoping to take Dream's mind off her injury.

"It's when you swim behind a boat in its waves. The faster the boat goes, the choppier the water gets. It's great fun." Dream managed a small smile.

"It's also dangerous if you get too close," said Star sharply. "We've warned you before to be careful. Now perhaps you'll listen to us."

As Star continued her lecture Antonia couldn't help but smile. Poor Dream. Star sounded so much like her own mother! When Star finally paused Antonia quickly changed the subject.

"Why are there dolphins circling us?"

"They're in our pod. They're protecting me. Blood attracts sharks," said Dream.

"It's just a precaution," said Star quickly. "There aren't any sharks here. Hush now, darling. You mustn't wear yourself out talking."

"*Muum!*" Dream flushed with embarrassment.

Antonia gave Dream a sympathetic look.

"I could really do with that seaweed," she said. "Star, will you go and look for some too?"

Star hesitated. "I suppose I could. You'll be all right, won't you, darling?"

"Of course I will," said Dream.

Star rubbed noses first with her daughter and then Antonia before swimming out of the dolphin ring. Antonia noticed Dream wince and was impressed by her bravery.

"Thanks," said Dream, when they were alone. "She was starting to drive me mad."

"My mum's the same," said Antonia. "They fuss because they care."

Her fingers were turning numb from pressing Dream's wound together. Carefully, Antonia flexed her fingers to get some life back in them. Blood spurted into the water. Gasping, Antonia held her fingers still.

"Is it really bad?" asked Dream.

Antonia hesitated, but Dream would expect her to tell the truth and she didn't want to break the dolphin's trust in her.

"It's not brilliant," she said at last. "But don't worry. Bubbles will be back soon. He's good at finding seaweed."

"I know," said Dream. "He's all right really, but don't tell him I said that."

Chapter Eleven

Antonia kept her fingers firmly pressed against Dream's wound. *Heal*, she thought, frightened by her inability to help the dolphin.

In her mind she imagined the wound closing up. First its sides would knit together. Then the blood would stop leaking. A picture formed in her head of Dream's damaged skin repairing itself. At once a warm feeling spread down Antonia's hands and into her fingers. Suddenly, her fingers began to prickle. The sensation hurt so badly Antonia wanted to pull her hands away. No! She had to keep her hands against Dream's wound. Gritting her teeth, Antonia continued to press down.

Heal! Antonia imagined Dream's soft skin re-growing, covering the wound. Dream trembled, but didn't make a sound.

Gradually the prickling lessened. Now it was more of an irritation. Antonia's hands still felt warm so she kept them pressed against Dream's soft skin until Dream cautiously said, "I've stopped hurting."

"Really?" asked Antonia in surprise.

Just then Spirit, followed by Star and

Bubbles slipped inside the dolphin circle. Their fins were covered in seaweed. Slowly Antonia lifted her hands away from Dream to inspect the wound. At first she could hardly believe her eyes. She looked again. The gash had healed, leaving a long scar with puckered edges.

"Silver Dolphin, that's amazing!"

Spirit stared at Antonia in awe. Then swimming forward he lightly touched the top of Antonia's head with his nose.

"Silver Dolphin, you are even more powerful than I imagined. We are very lucky to have you with us."

"But…" Antonia stared at Dream's scar in disbelief. "How did… that wasn't me, was it?"

"Who else?" Spirit smiled. "It is rare for a Silver Dolphin to have the power to heal. I know only of one other who can do this."

"Claudia," said Antonia at once.

Spirit nodded and Antonia felt a sudden rush of pride. Claudia was so good with injured animals. Could she really be that good herself?

"Hey, Flipper Feet, that's so bubbly," squealed Bubbles, turning a somersault.

"Steady, Bubbles," Star warned him. "Your sister needs time to recover. She's had a nasty shock."

"It's all right, Mum," said Dream. "Bubbles is cool. He's had a shock too."

"Can we play?" asked Bubbles. "Seaweed tag." He flipped the long strand of seaweed draped over his flipper at Antonia.

"Not now, Bubbles," said Spirit. "Your mother is right. Dream should rest. Besides, the Silver Dolphin must go home. You can play another time."

Antonia wasn't sure if she had the energy to go anywhere. She felt exhausted. Her arms ached and her fingers still tingled. It was peaceful inside the dolphin circle. She wished she could stay there longer.

"Do you need help?" asked Spirit. "Two of my dolphins can tow you some of the way."

Antonia pulled herself together. "I can manage," she said.

Spirit nodded approvingly.

"I'll swim some of the way with you," he said. "No, Bubbles, you can't come this time. Stay with your sister and don't annoy her too much."

"As if!" clicked Bubbles, pulling a face and making everyone laugh.

Antonia felt slightly awkward saying goodbye. Star especially made a huge fuss of her, rubbing her nose against Antonia's nose and stroking her hair with a flipper.

"Thanks, Silver Dolphin," said Dream, lightly tapping her fin against Antonia's hand in a gesture of friendship.

"Flipper Feet!" clicked Bubbles, high-fiving Antonia with his fin. "Seaweed tag next time."

"You're on," said Antonia, high-fiving him back.

Spirit swam with Antonia as close to the *Princess Romana* as he dared. Then he turned to look at her, his liquid eyes serious.

"Take care, Silver Dolphin. Remember we

are secret friends. There are many who seek magic for their own gain and their greed causes nothing but harm."

"Our secret is safe," said Antonia, solemnly placing a hand on Spirit's fin. "I promise that I'll be careful."

They stared at each other in silence until Spirit dipped his head, then lightly ruffling Antonia's hair with a flipper, he dived under the water and was gone. Antonia lay on her back feeling the vibrations in the water lessen as Spirit swam further away. When they were no more than a whisper she dived down and swam halfway back to Claudia's beach underwater.

Reaching the shore, Antonia felt like sinking down on the sand and falling asleep. Her muscles ached and it was a struggle to keep her eyes open. She forced herself on, not daring to sit as she recovered her swimming bag from the Sea Watch boat and pulled on her shoes.

Antonia loved the light summer evenings, but tonight, as she crept into Claudia's garden, she longed for the dark. Nervously she glanced up at the house and then she froze. Cai stood at an upstairs window looking out to sea. If he looked down now he would be able to see her. Antonia pressed herself into the shrubs and stood like a statue. The seconds ticked by. Antonia willed Cai to move away from the window, but to her horror he suddenly turned to the garden and looked straight at her. Antonia felt her heart fall to her feet. She could see Cai clearly, but could he see her in the shadows?

Then a second figure came up behind Cai. It was Claudia, stepping forward and swiftly drawing the curtains. Antonia was grateful that Claudia still kept in touch with the dolphins. She must have guessed that Antonia would use her beach to answer their call. But had Cai seen her or not?

Antonia's stomach churned with worry as she scurried alongside the house and out into the street. What would she say if he'd seen her? She would have to make up an excuse. She hated the thought of fibbing to Cai, but knew she might have to. Becoming a Silver Dolphin was the most wonderful thing that had happened to her. She couldn't break her promise to the dolphins. Touching her charm for comfort, Antonia forced her tired legs to carry her back to the swimming pool.

When she was almost there she pulled Dad's mobile phone out of her bag and called up 'home' in the address book. She was about to press the Send button when she noticed a blue people carrier parked outside the swimming-pool doors. Antonia's heart raced. Nothing was going right for her. The car belonged to her dad. He must have come early to watch her swim.

Stuffing the mobile phone back in her bag Antonia broke into a run. Her throat went dry as she imagined Dad seeking out one of the coaches to ask why his daughter wasn't in the swimming pool. Both Mum and Dad had strict rules about her going out. At this time in the evening she was only allowed to take part in organised activities.

Out of breath, Antonia arrived at the swimming-pool entrance. She made herself stand outside until she'd stopped panting then, wiping sweaty palms down her leggings, she went in. The reception hall was empty except for the lady she'd seen earlier at the desk. Luckily she was tapping away at a computer and didn't notice Antonia heading towards the spectators' door. Feeling sick with fear Antonia pushed the door open at exactly the same time as someone came through it from the other side.

"Oh!" gasped Antonia, her face flushing a guilty shade of red as she faced her dad.

"There you are." Dad sounded relieved. "Why aren't you in the pool with everyone else?"

Antonia linked her arm through Dad's and steered him outside.

"I was allowed to get out early as it's my first time."

"Was it fun?" asked Dad, unlocking the car door.

Antonia hugged her swimming bag close to her chest. Fun didn't even begin to describe the adventures she'd had this evening. Giving her dad a huge smile she said, "I've had an amazing time."

Chapter Twelve

At school everyone was very excited. The damaged *Princess Romana* had been repaired and the boat was due to sail that afternoon. Mr Cordier decided that the whole school should go down to the promenade to wave her off. Only Sophie wasn't happy about the news.

"It can't leave yet. I haven't finished my picture," she wailed.

"Take your sketch pad with you and you can do some more drawing before the ship sails," Antonia suggested, knowing that Sophie always brought her sketch pad to school.

"I suppose I could, but it won't be the same," said Sophie glumly. "I can't concentrate with too many people around."

Antonia laughed. "Once you get started you'll soon forget everyone. You go into your own little world when you're drawing."

Antonia was right. In fact, Sophie became dreamy and distracted as soon as she decided that she'd take her sketch pad on their outing to the beach. In English she did all her work in her maths book by mistake. Miss Brown was so cross she made Sophie stay in at playtime to copy the work out in her English book. Antonia was dismayed. She'd managed to avoid being alone with Cai all morning, but it would be more difficult with no Sophie to hang around with in the playground. She needn't have worried. Cai didn't seem to want to be alone with her either and ran off to play football with the boys. Miserably, Antonia sat on the edge of the field watching everyone having fun around her. She hated avoiding Cai, but what if he had seen her the night before and asked about it? However she explained herself Cai would know she was keeping secrets from him. Lunchtime was a little better. Cai, Toby, Sophie and Antonia sat together on the field to eat their sandwiches.

"It'll be good to see the back of the *Princess Romana*," said Cai. "I used to see dolphins swimming in the bay, but they haven't been around since that boat's been stuck here."

Antonia choked on a mouthful of sandwich.

"Steady," said Cai, thumping her on the back. "Are you all right? You've gone a funny colour."

"I'm fine," spluttered Antonia.

She took a long swig from her drink bottle, then wiped her mouth with the back of her hand. She would have to learn to control herself and not start acting funnily if Cai mentioned dolphins again.

"The beaches are opening again tomorrow," said Toby. "The coastguard told Mum that the oil has almost gone and that most of the stuff washed up has been cleared away. The funniest thing they found was a whole crate of false teeth. Some of the teeth had dead fish stuck between them like they were having a snack."

"I bet you made that up!" said Cai when the laughter died down.

"Would I lie to you?" Toby grinned.

"Yes, you would," said Cai, looking at Antonia. She felt her face colouring up. Cai started unwrapping a slice of cake.

"Mmm," he said appreciatively. "It's not like I don't miss my parents or anything, but Aunty Claudia is a much better cook. Did you ask about staying to tea tonight, Antonia? We're having homemade pasta."

"Yes, I can come," said Antonia, pleased

that he still wanted her to go.

Biting into her apple Antonia decided she was worrying about nothing. Cai was still being friendly so he couldn't have seen her last night.

After lunch Miss Brown made the class line up in pairs to go down to the promenade. It was crowded with onlookers so the police allowed the children of Sandy Bay Primary to go down on to the sand. The *Princess Romana* was flying several flags, including the Union Jack, alongside its own green, white and red striped Italian one.

"Doesn't it look pretty?" said Sophie, pulling out her sketch pad. "I can't wait to paint this."

The crew lined the deck and when the boat

began to sail they released a hundred green, white and red balloons into the air. Antonia cheered almost as loudly as the whole school put together. The beach was almost cleared and the oil spill had nearly dispersed so it wouldn't be long before Spirit and his family could return to the bay. Suddenly, Antonia was so excited she did a little dance in the sand.

"Antonia!" cried Sophie, brushing sand from her sketch pad. "Watch out!"

"Sorry," said Antonia, standing still again. "Wow, Sophie, that's brilliant."

"It's not bad," said Sophie, rapidly sketching. "I could have done with longer, though."

After school Antonia walked to Sea Watch with Cai, Eleanor and Karen. As they entered the Sea Watch building Claudia drew Antonia to one side.

"I need a word with you," she whispered.

Panic gripped Antonia, making her grey-green eyes widen in alarm.

"You're not in any trouble." Claudia squeezed Antonia's hand. "It's good news. I'll talk to you later."

Antonia and Cai offered to clean out the guillemot cages. They were in the back room, nine birds in three cages. The survivors were a tough, cheeky bunch and Antonia was growing fond of them. Donning large rubber gloves Antonia and Cai rolled up soiled newspaper and replaced it with clean stuff. They refreshed water dishes and finally refilled the plastic food cartons with fish.

"They're very greedy," said Cai, watching the largest bird wolf down a herring.

"They sound like cats." The guillemots made a soft purring noise that made Antonia laugh. She was so absorbed watching them that she was only half aware of a tickling feeling on her neck. She rubbed at it and her fingers brushed against her dolphin charm. Suddenly, Antonia realised the charm was vibrating.

Spirit, she thought, only just stopping the words from escaping out loud.

"I'll put the rubbish out if you sweep the floor," said Cai, picking up the dustbin bag.

"No, I'll put the rubbish out," said Antonia forcefully.

Cai gave her a quizzical look. "All right," he said. "If you're that keen to do it then go ahead."

"Yes, no, I mean…" Realising she was babbling, Antonia clamped her mouth shut.

She grabbed the dustbin bag from Cai, glad of an excuse to escape. The dolphin charm was vibrating strongly and Antonia was desperate to answer the call. Was Dream in trouble again? What if Antonia hadn't healed her properly and the wound had turned bad? She wrenched the outside door open.

A shrill whistle burst from Antonia's necklace followed by a series of clicks.

"Wait," said Cai, holding her arm. "What's that noise?"

Antonia stared at Cai in disbelief. Surely he

didn't mean the noise coming from her necklace? Only a Silver Dolphin could hear that.

"What noise?" she asked, pulling her arm free.

"I thought I heard a whistle."

"I didn't hear it," said Antonia, backing out of the door.

Cai followed, a dazed look on his face. Antonia wondered how to get rid of him when suddenly there was Claudia.

"Antonia," she said, winking. "Can you put that rubbish out on you own? I've another job for Cai."

Antonia nodded, gratefully escaping as Claudia steered Cai in the opposite direction.

Chapter Thirteen

 ntonia dumped the rubbish in the wheelie bin, then hurtled through the gate that led to the beach. Quickly she pulled off her shoes, throwing them into the Sea Watch boat as she passed.

"Spirit, I'm coming," she panted.

Soft white sand flew up in her face as she

raced down to the water. She splashed into the sea and when she was in waist deep she swam, thrilling as her legs melded together like a tail. Antonia leapt in and out of the water, skimming across its surface as she hurried to answer Spirit's call. It felt like flying, but she was too anxious to enjoy it. Sandy Bay was empty now the *Princess Romana* had gone. The sea stretched away, rippling like a huge blue flag in the breeze. Antonia hurtled on, swimming until she felt vibrations in the water and saw four dolphins coming towards her. Then she slowed. Three of the dolphins held back allowing the second smallest dolphin to lead the way. It was Dream. Shyly she swam up to Antonia and hesitantly greeted her, nose to nose.

Antonia held her breath as she gently rubbed the dolphin's nose back.

"Hello, Dream, are you better now?"

Dream dipped her silver head. "Yes, thanks to you. I'll always be grateful to you for healing me, Silver Dolphin."

Antonia blushed, for once tongue-tied. Spirit, Star and Bubbles swam forward.

"We'll always be grateful too," said Spirit.

"It was nothing," clicked Antonia. "I was glad I could help."

Spirit patted Antonia's head with his fin. "We need your help again, Silver Dolphin. The dolphins in my pod keep finding funny coloured things floating in the sea. Can you take them back to shore so they're not mistaken for food?"

"Look, Silver Dolphin!" Bubbles exclaimed. "There's one there, the green thing that's a bit like seaweed."

"It's a burst balloon," said Antonia. "It's come from the *Princess Romana*. The sailors released a hundred coloured balloons when they sailed from Sandy Bay."

"Was that the boat caught in the storm?" asked Spirit.

Antonia nodded. "I don't suppose the sailors realised the harm they could cause by letting the balloons go. They wouldn't have wanted that, especially after the damage they'd already done to the sea."

Spirit nodded. "Pollution is often caused in error," he clicked.

"Dad, can I help the Silver Dolphin to find

the balloons?" asked Dream.

"And me," squeaked Bubbles, rolling in the water.

Antonia held her breath. It was the first time Dream had offered to help. She hoped that Bubbles's exuberance wouldn't put her off like it usually did.

"Yes, you can. It's a good idea," said Spirit.

"Thanks, Dad. Are you ready, Silver Dolphin?" Dream asked shyly.

Antonia's smile was a metre wide. At last she felt that Dream might become her friend.

"Be careful, my darlings," warned Star. "Don't accidentally swallow the balloons."

"*Muuum*," clicked Dream. "Don't fuss!"

Antonia, Dream and Bubbles swam round collecting up the burst balloons. Antonia shuddered each time she picked one up. They felt limp and slimy and they reminded her of jellyfish. Antonia was allergic to jellyfish and used to be very frightened of them until she'd learnt how to avoid them. When all the balloons had been recovered Antonia wrapped them into a ball with the ribbon attached to them, then tied the ball to her wrist. The balloon ball was so light it would be easy to carry home to dispose of properly.

"We're done!" clicked Bubbles cheerfully. "Come on, Flipper Feet. Let's ask Dad if we can play."

Antonia was about to follow Bubbles when she realised that Dream wasn't with them. Neatly somersaulting in the water she went back for her.

"Will you play with us?" she asked.

Dream hesitated.

"Please?"

"Thanks. I'd like that." clicked Dream.

Bubbles reached his parents ahead of everyone else, but before he could speak Spirit silenced him.

"Something's swimming this way," he said.

Antonia could sense it too. Intrigued, she trod water. The vibrations were really strong. The approaching animal must be quite big.

"It feels like…" Spirit tensed. "I don't believe it! But how can that be?"

His bright eyes scanned the water, widening as the splashing shape came into focus.

"Impossible," he whistled.

Following his gaze Antonia wondered if she

was dreaming. Surely that wasn't Cai hesitantly swimming closer? Realising it was, Antonia's mouth opened in surprise. How on earth had Cai managed to swim out so far? Surprise quickly turned to fear. Cai must have followed her.

"Spirit, I'm sorry. It's my fault. I tried my best to keep our friendship a secret..."

Spirit wasn't listening. Instead he swam forward to greet Cai.

"Silver Dolphin," he clicked in wonder. "You answered the dolphin's call."

"But what's..." Cai's voice squeaked, then stopped. He cleared his throat. "What's happening to me?" he clicked at last. "What's a Silver Dolphin?"

"A Silver Dolphin is someone who cares for

the sea and all the dolphins and creatures that live here," said Spirit kindly. "A Silver Dolphin must answer the dolphins' call to give help whenever it is needed."

Cai stared at Spirit with astonishment.

"Aunty Claudia said something about answering the call when she lent me this." He held out his hand. Wrapped around his wrist was a silver chain with a dolphin charm.

"Claudia is a very special friend," clicked Spirit. "I can hardly believe that she's found us a second Silver Dolphin. Silver Dolphins are very rare."

Suddenly Cai noticed Antonia bobbing excitedly in the water.

"Are you a Silver Dolphin too?" he asked.

Antonia's smile mirrored Cai's.

"Yes," she said.

"That's so cool!" Cai accidentally lapsed into his human voice.

Impatiently Bubbles tapped Antonia on the shoulder.

"What's he saying?"

Antonia laughed. "You have to speak dolphin," she clicked.

"How?"

"It's easy when you get the hang of it. Just believe you're a dolphin and let it happen."

"What... like this?" Cai whistled and clicked. Suddenly, he burst out laughing. "This is so amazing!" Pinching himself, he laughed again. "Ouch! Definitely not dreaming then!"

"Two Silver Dolphins, that's so bubbly," whistled Bubbles. "Can we play, Dad? Can we teach the new Silver Dolphin seaweed tag?"

Indulgently, Spirit patted Bubbles on the head with his flipper.

"Next time," he promised. "Give the new Silver Dolphin a chance to take all this in."

"Please?" Bubbles begged.

"Bubbles," warned Star.

"Can I swim some of the way home with the Silver Dolphins then?" asked Bubbles.

"Yes," Spirit nodded. "Just don't go too close to the shore."

"Bubbly!" Bubbles leapt up and, standing on his tail on the sea's surface, turned a full circle.

"Bubbles!" shrieked Dream as he splashed down and soaked everyone.

Spirit and Star said goodbye, gently rubbing noses with Cai and Antonia. Cai was so excited it reminded Antonia of how she felt when she'd first learnt she was a Silver Dolphin. She hung back, letting Cai swim alongside Bubbles.

"Are you coming too?" she asked Dream.

Dream looked undecided and Antonia held her breath, hoping she would agree.

"Yes, I'll come," she clicked at last.

"That's bubbly!" Antonia lightly brushed Dream's nose with her own.

They swam together, a short distance behind Cai and Bubbles. Antonia watched them fondly. She could hardly believe that Cai was a Silver Dolphin too.

I need a word with you.

From nowhere Claudia's words from earlier whispered round Antonia's head. Claudia must have been going to tell her that Cai could be a Silver Dolphin!

"Hey, Flipper Feet," Bubbles slowed up. "He's doing that funny thing you used to do with your arms."

Cai's legs flicked at the water, working together like a tail, but his arms swam breaststroke.

Antonia laughed.

"Give him a chance," she clicked back. "Remember he's only just discovered he's a Silver Dolphin."

A shiver of excitement tingled through Antonia. Two Silver Dolphins! Think of the difference to the environment they could make! But best of all was having Cai as part of the amazing secret too. Now they could share everything.

Use your magic wisely, Silver Dolphin, said Claudia's voice in her head.

I will, Antonia promised back.

Bubbles and Cai pulled ahead so Antonia sped up.

"Come on, Dream," she whistled. "We can't let the boys beat us. Let's race them."

Silver Dolphins
by Summer Waters

Buy more great Silver Dolphins books from HarperCollins at 10% off recommended retail price. FREE postage and packing in the UK.

Out Now:

Silver Dolphins – The Magic Charm   ISBN: 978-0-00-730968-9

Silver Dolphins – Secret Friends   ISBN: 978-0-00-730969-6

Coming soon:

Silver Dolphins – Stolen Treasures   ISBN: 978-0-00-730970-2

Silver Dolphins – Double Danger   ISBN: 978-0-00-730971-9

Silver Dolphins – Broken Promises   ISBN: 978-0-00-730972-6

Silver Dolphins – Moonlight Magic   ISBN: 978-0-00-730973-3

All priced at £4.99